This edition published by Parragon Books Ltd in 2017

Parragon Books Ltd
Chartist House
15–17 Trim Street
Bath BA1 1HA, UK
www.parragon.com

ISBN 978-1-4748-7446-5

Printed in China

BATMAN

PaRragon

Bath • New York • Cologne • Melbourne • Delhi
Hong Kong • Shenzhen • Singapore

Batman was in the Batcave with
Robin when they saw the news –
a famous doctor had been kidnapped!
"To the Batmobile!" Batman cried.

Batman and Robin rushed to the Batmobile and drove straight to the doctor's office, where some police officers were already on the scene.

The room had been ransacked. Batman looked at the claw marks everywhere and suddenly realized who was behind this crime.

"Killer Croc," he told the police.

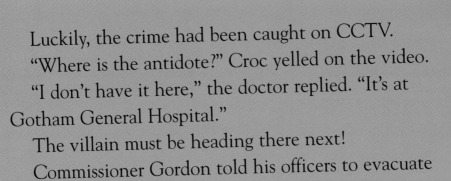

Luckily, the crime had been caught on CCTV.

"Where is the antidote?" Croc yelled on the video.

"I don't have it here," the doctor replied. "It's at Gotham General Hospital."

The villain must be heading there next!

Commissioner Gordon told his officers to evacuate the hospital – Batman was going to set a trap.

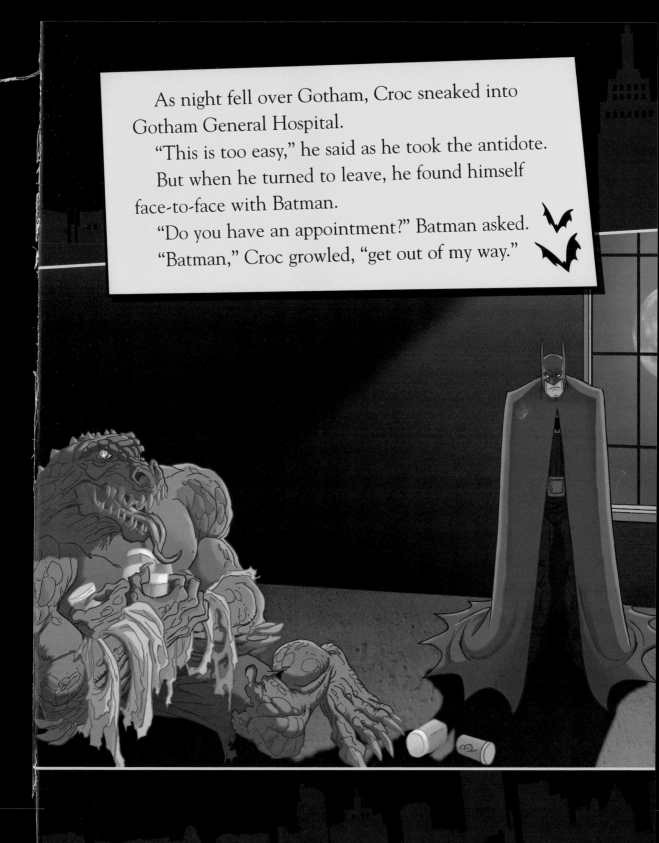

As night fell over Gotham, Croc sneaked into Gotham General Hospital.

"This is too easy," he said as he took the antidote.

But when he turned to leave, he found himself face-to-face with Batman.

"Do you have an appointment?" Batman asked.

"Batman," Croc growled, "get out of my way."

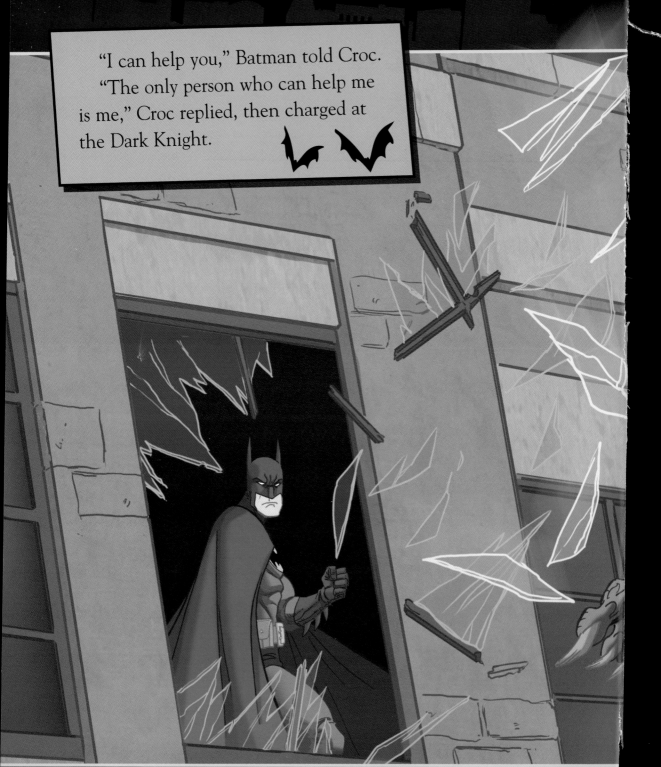

Croc was strong, but Batman was fast. He moved out of the way just as Croc reached him. Croc couldn't stop in time and so he crashed through a window, out of the hospital!

Croc landed safely on the street below.
He looked back once at Batman, before
disappearing into the sewers.

"You let him get away!" Commissioner Gordon cried, when Batman returned empty-handed.

"No, I didn't," replied Batman.

He held up a small screen showing a flashing red dot – he had hidden a tracking device on Croc's scaly skin.

"He'll take us right to the doctor," said Batman.

"How will you follow him in the sewers?" asked the commissioner.

"I can help with that," said a voice.

Robin was standing in the doorway holding two scuba suits!

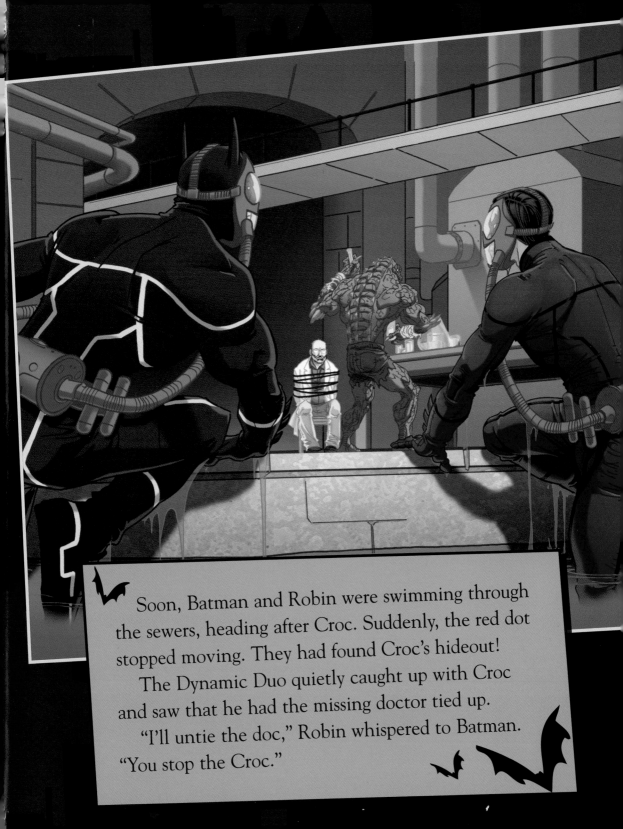

Soon, Batman and Robin were swimming through the sewers, heading after Croc. Suddenly, the red dot stopped moving. They had found Croc's hideout!

The Dynamic Duo quietly caught up with Croc and saw that he had the missing doctor tied up.

"I'll untie the doc," Robin whispered to Batman. "You stop the Croc."

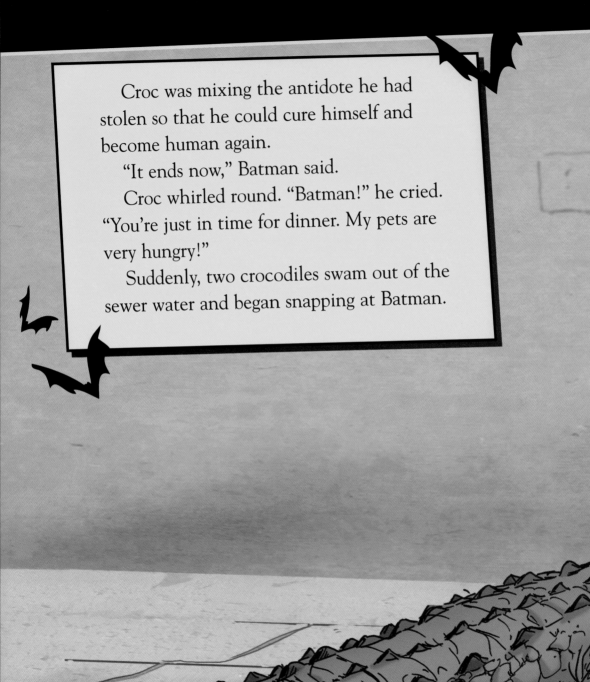

Croc was mixing the antidote he had stolen so that he could cure himself and become human again.

"It ends now," Batman said.

Croc whirled round. "Batman!" he cried. "You're just in time for dinner. My pets are very hungry!"

Suddenly, two crocodiles swam out of the sewer water and began snapping at Batman.

Killer Croc ran away as his crocodiles attacked Batman. But the Caped Crusader kept his cool. He reached for the reptile repellent in his Utility Belt and sprayed the beasts, who quickly fell asleep.

Meanwhile, Robin had rescued the doctor.
The trio caught up with Croc.
"You can't beat me, Batman!" Croc cried.
"I'm here to help you," Batman said.
"There are good doctors in prison."

"No one's ever helped me before. Why would they start now?" Croc yelled, and then lunged at Batman. But the Caped Crusader was ready.

The pair wrestled and Batman fought to keep himself out of Croc's fearsome jaws. He needed some help!

Robin grabbed Croc's antidote.
"You want this, Lizard Lips?" Robin yelled.
"Come and get it!"
"No!" Croc screamed, as Robin threw the antidote into the sewer water. Croc dived in after the bottles.

Batman made sure the doctor was okay before he and Robin dived in after Croc. Croc found the bottles, but then discovered he had company!

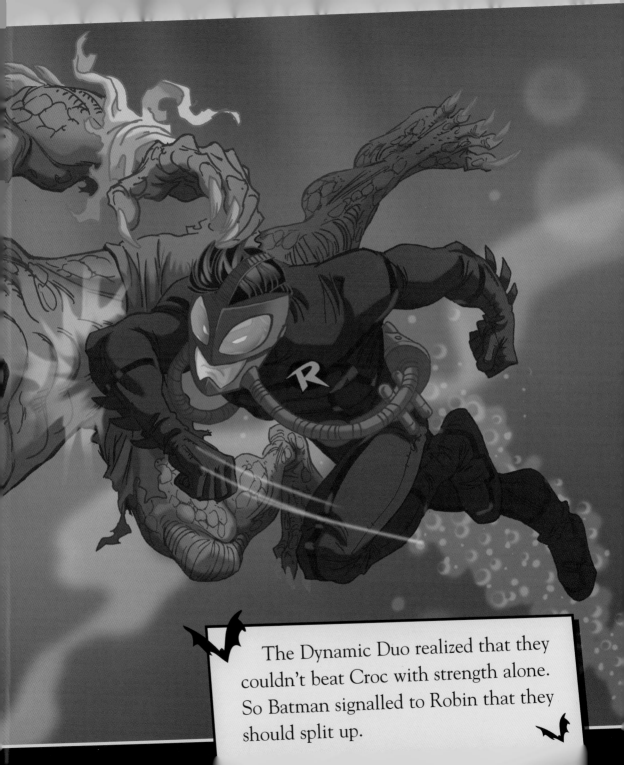

The Dynamic Duo realized that they couldn't beat Croc with strength alone. So Batman signalled to Robin that they should split up.

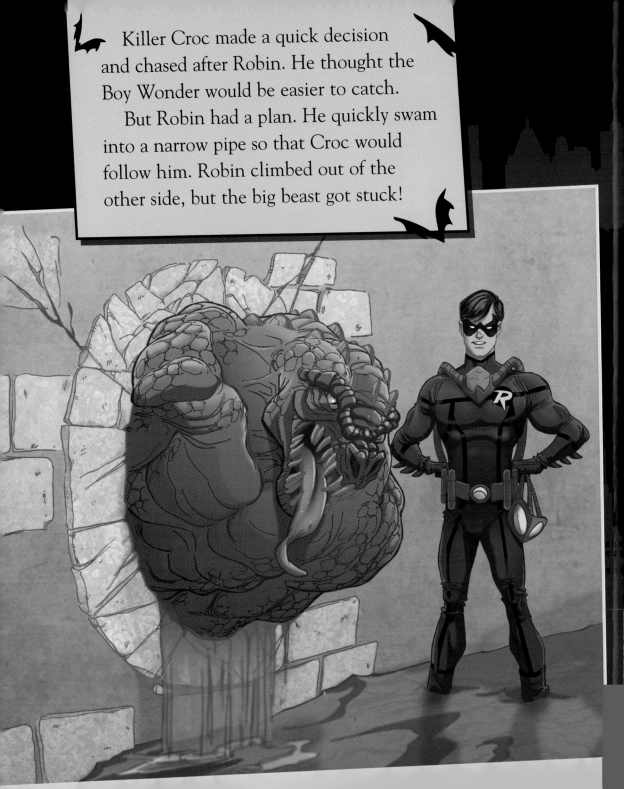

Killer Croc made a quick decision and chased after Robin. He thought the Boy Wonder would be easier to catch.

But Robin had a plan. He quickly swam into a narrow pipe so that Croc would follow him. Robin climbed out of the other side, but the big beast got stuck!

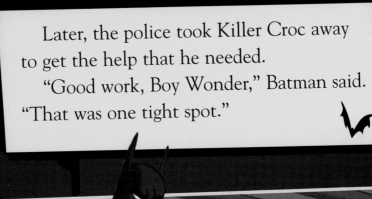

Later, the police took Killer Croc away to get the help that he needed.

"Good work, Boy Wonder," Batman said.

"That was one tight spot."